DANNY McGEE

DRINKS THE SEA

ANDY STANTON & NEAL LAYTON

DANNY McGEE
DRINKS THE SEA

For Alex and Asher, with love A.S.
For Betsy and Erica N.L.

HODDER CHILDREN'S BOOKS

First published in Great Britain in 2016 by Hodder and Stoughton
This edition published in 2017 by Hodder and Stoughton

Text copyright © Andy Stanton 2016
Illustration copyright © Neal Layton 2016
Additional photography by
Anthony 'Shutterbug' McGowan

Hodder Children's Books
An imprint of Hachette Children's Group
Part of Hodder and Stoughton
Carmelite House, 50 Victoria Embankment
London EC4 0DZ

The right of Andy Stanton to be identified as the author and Neal Layton as the illustrator
of this Work has been asserted by them in accordance with the Copyright, Designs and Patents Act 1988.

A CIP catalogue record for this book is available from the British Library.

ISBN: 978 1 444 92878 5
10 9 8 7 6 5 4 3 2 1

Printed in China

Hodder
Children's
Books

FSC
www.fsc.org

MIX
Paper from
responsible sources
FSC® C104740

One summer's day, Danny
and Frannie McGee
hopped into a car
and drove down
to the sea.

The sea was all sparkly,
blue as can be...

'I bet I can drink it,'
said Danny McGee.

Said Frannie, 'No, Danny,
I cannot **agree**,
you'll **never** drink all of it,
Danny McGee.'

'I will, just you watch,'
replied Danny McGee,
'Please fetch me a straw
and then you will see.'

So Fran fetched a straw that was longer than she...

In ten minutes' time
there was no sea to see,

because all of the sea
was in Danny McGee.

And he swallowed a **bird**

and he swallowed a **bee**

and he swallowed a **cat**
who was drinking some tea.

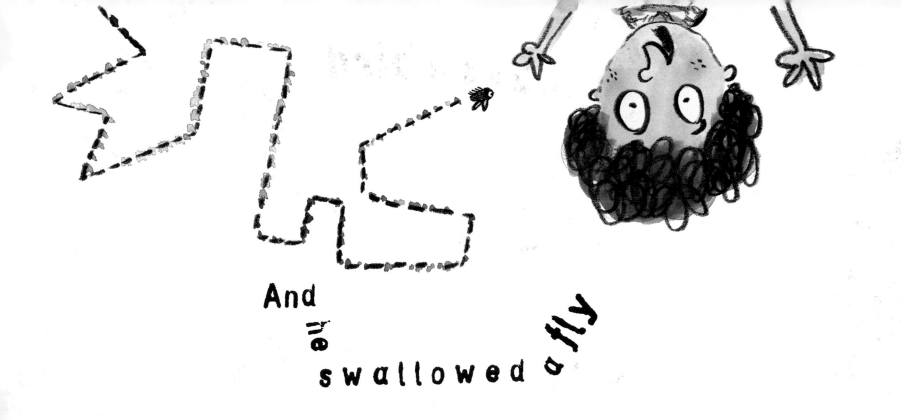

And he swallowed a fly

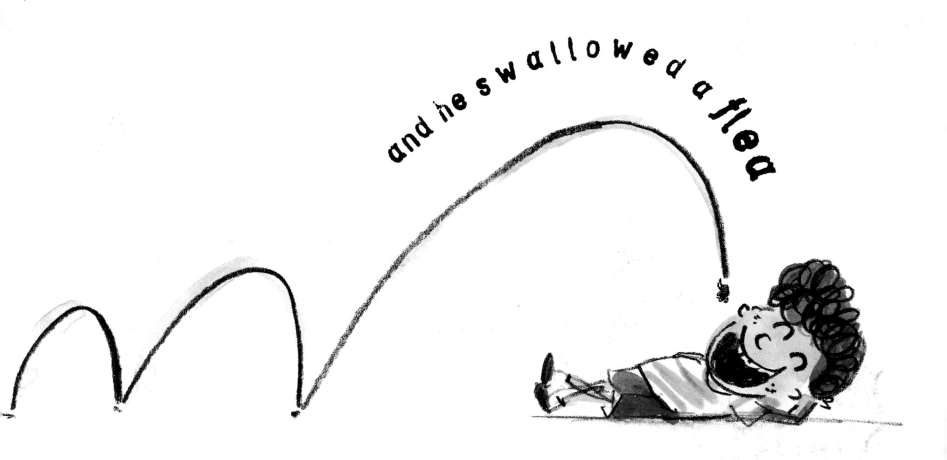

and he swallowed a flea

and he swallowed a man

who was learning to ski.

And he swallowed a pie

and he swallowed a pea

and he swallowed the weather girl on the **TV**.

'You're naughty!' said Frannie,
'I'm telling, you'll see!'
But Danny just giggled...

tee hee!

and swallowed a **swee.**

And I know you think there's
no such thing as a swee,
but believe me, there **was**,
before Danny McGee.

S is for "Swee"

The Swee is a hairy
sort of fellow na ive
the upper lower easter
regions of the Wester
Northlands of the
South. Little is known
about these remarke
except that

'I will swallow it all!'
shouted Danny McGee,
and he swallowed the sand
where the sea used to be.

And he swallowed
the **mountains**,

and every last **tree**,

and he swallowed the jungles, he did it with glee.

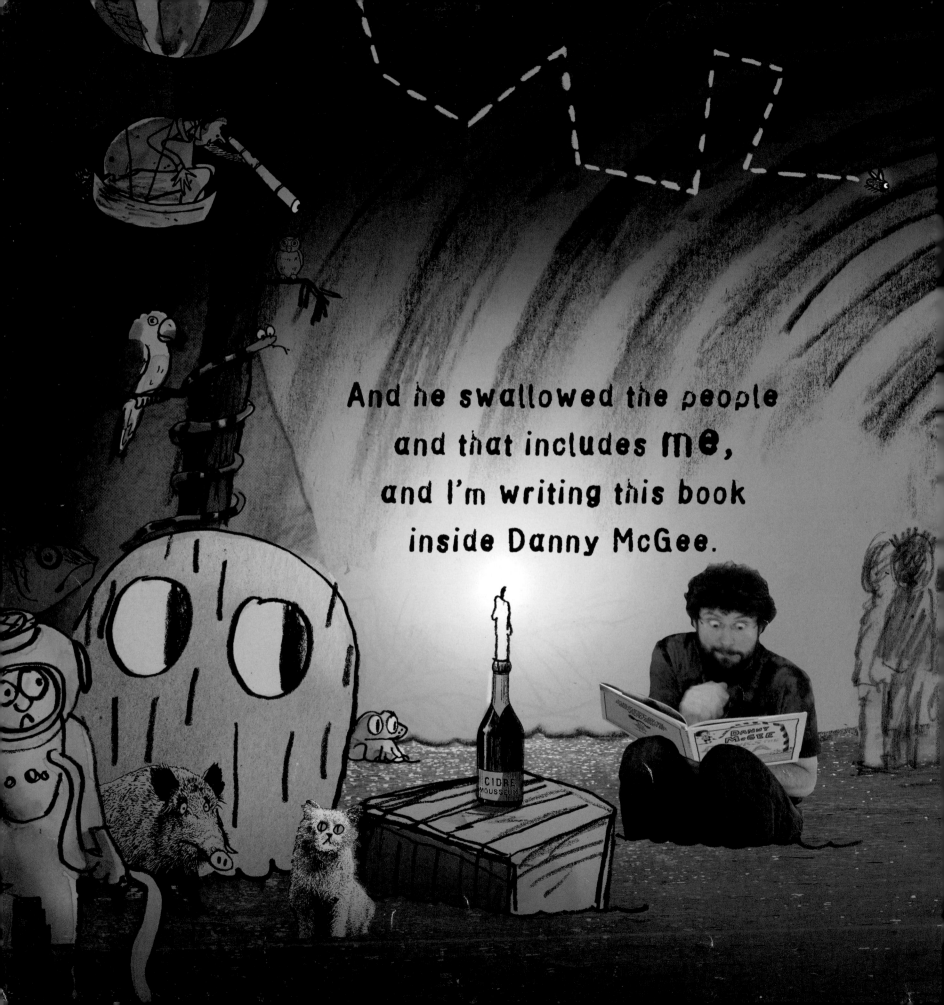

And he swallowed the people
and that includes **me**,
and I'm writing this book
inside Danny McGee.

And he swallowed America,
land of the free,

and he swallowed up London,
chim chim cher-ee!

'Danny, you didn't get me.'

And she opened her mouth
and **s w a l l o w e d**

Danny McGee.